If the Shoe Fits

Lalie Harcourt & Ricki Wortzman

Illustrated by Steve Attoe

🔁 Dominie Press, Inc.

Prince Peter had the blues.

It was time to go out,
but where were his shoes?

3

The maid ran in.

"I found these," she said.

"They were hard to see under the bed.

Do they fit?"

The prince turned the shoes
from side to side.
"Oh, no," he said, "these are too wide."

5

The king ran in.
"I found these," he said.
"They were in the closet above my head.
Do they fit?"

6

The prince looked at the shoes
with the heel so tall.
"Oh, no," he said, "these are too small."

7

The guard ran in.

"I found these," she said.

"They were at the very back of the shed.
Do they fit?"

The prince looked at the shoes
with points like an arrow.
"Oh, no," he said, "these are too narrow."

9

The cook ran in.
"I found these," he said.
"They were in the drawer
with the freshly baked bread.
Do they fit?"

The prince looked at the shoes
as he sang a song.
"Oh, no," he said, "these are too long."

The queen ran in.

"I found these," she said.

"They were in my sewing kit near the thread. Do they fit?"

The prince looked at the shoes under the light.
"Oh, no," he said, "these are too tight."

In ran the dog.
In his mouth were some shoes.

14

Would these be the ones
to fix Prince Peter's blues?

Peter tried on the shoes
as he looked at the dog.
"This pair fits!" he said.
"Let's go for a jog!"